Henrietta
and the Perfect Night

Henrietta
and the Perfect Night

Martine Murray

ALLEN&UNWIN
SYDNEY · MELBOURNE · AUCKLAND · LONDON

To the possum M.M.

First published by Allen & Unwin in 2017

Allen & Unwin
83 Alexander Street
Crows Nest NSW 2065
Australia
Phone: (61 2) 8425 0100
Email: info@allenandunwin.com
Web: www.allenandunwin.com

A Cataloguing-in-Publication entry is available
from the National Library of Australia
www.trove.nla.gov.au

ISBN 978 1 76029 024 5

Cover and text illustrations by Martine Murray
Cover and text design by Sandra Nobes
Set in 15 pt Jenson Classico by Sandra Nobes

This book was printed in November 2016 by
Hang Tai Printing Company Limited, China.

1 3 5 7 9 10 8 6 4 2

Contents

The Waiting Game

Hello, I'm Henrietta the Great Go-Getter. I'm also a Big Thinker. And right now I'm thinking about my mum getting fat. This sometimes happens to mums and dads. Dads also lose the hair on their head. Poor dads. I wouldn't like to lose my hair because it's good for making up hairstyles. Like this.

All kinds of things change with mums and dads. Hair goes grey. Noses get bigger. Wrinkles and crinkles appear. But inside they're still your mum and dad who love you. And I don't mind one bit if they change on the outside.

My mum isn't really getting fat. It's just that there's a baby growing inside her and one day it will come out.

'What sort of baby?' I ask.

'We don't know yet.'

'Will it be a nice one?'

'All babies are nice.'

'A little sister?'

'Maybe, or a little brother. We'll have to wait and see.'

I'm terrible at waiting.

Mum says I must learn to be patient.
But I say there are more exciting things
to learn than patience. Like how to
fly to the moon. How to tap dance.
How to cook pavlova. Patience
is for flowers in the field,
and teachers of little kids,
and for mums.

What's more, I already know I want a
baby sister, not a baby brother. What can
you do with brothers? Boys are bossy and
noisy. But a little sister – she'll smell just
right, like roses and sweets and streams and
kittens. She'll love tap dancing, and I'll carry
her everywhere and dress her up in different
sorts of hats, and one day I'll teach her how
to catch bugs, and how to play snap. I may
even let her win. Sometimes.

'How much longer do I have to wait for my baby sister?' I say.

'Six more months,' says Dad.

'How long is six months?'

'Half way to Christmas.'

'That's a lot of waiting!'

'That's because the baby needs to be properly cooked.'

'Dad, it's not a cake, it's a baby.'

Sometimes my dad forgets what's what. Lucky I'm here to put him straight.

'You're right, it isn't a cake. But, speaking of cakes, since we have to wait six months for a baby and only half an hour for a cake, how about we bake a chocolate ripple cake right now?'

Who says no to cake? Not me. But I've had chocolate ripple cake before and it didn't make me patient. I'm not convinced it will make me patient now. Cake or no cake, I have discoveries to make.

'But, Dad, why does it take so long to grow a baby?'

'Because at first a baby is as small as a seed in the ground, only it's a seed inside a mum. And you know how long it takes for a seed to grow.'

I have a think about this.

I already happen to know that seeds are slow, and they need sun and water and loving care, because we planted sunflowers and I had to dribble the hose on them carefully whenever it was hot. But you can't water a seed inside your mum's tummy, or show it the sun.

'But what makes the seed inside Mum grow?' I ask my dad.

Dad has a think about this. My dad's a big thinker, like me.

'Daddy's love started it going, and Mum's body keeps it growing,' he says. Then he takes me outside.

'See the apple tree? Once, that tree was just a seed in the ground, and now it's big enough to grow apples. By the end of summer those apples will be big enough for apple crumble. Do you know what season it will be when we eat apple crumble?'

'Autumn!' I say.

'Yes, autumn, when the leaves change colour and drop off. Then comes winter, when there's no fruit or leaves, just the cold, bare branches. But once little buds start growing again, then you'll know it's time for the baby to come.'

'In spring?'

'Yes, in spring.'

So, when buds show on the apple tree, my waiting will be over. Finally.

Still, that's a very long time,

and still I have no patience.

The very next day I check the apples to see if they've grown bigger, but they haven't. I'm worried. This will take a very long time if they don't start growing soon. Maybe they forgot to grow. Or maybe they need loving care.

I could kiss them, but it would be too hard to kiss the ones up high, and you can't really have favourites. That wouldn't be fair.

And there are so many apples to give
presents to, and so many to whisper kind
words to. I have an idea. I'll sing them
a lullaby. That's how Mum gets me
to sleep. I go and find Mum's
ukulele, then I climb up the tree.

Only I don't know how to play the
ukulele. It's harder than I thought, but surely
not too hard. I climb down again and run
inside. Dad is baking his cake and Mum has
put her feet up.

I say, 'Can you show me how to play a song for the apples?'

'Why do you want to play a song for the apples?' says Mum.

'Because I want to give them some loving care, so they grow faster, so the tree loses its leaves faster, and then it will soon be time for the baby to come.'

'Good idea,' says Mum.

So we go outside and sit under the tree together, and Mum tries to teach me to play the ukulele. But after a while I say she can play and I'll sing, as I have no patience for learning to play the ukulele but I do have a mouth to sing with.

Everyone does. (Except worms. Poor worms. They can't sing. And maybe fish can't sing, either, since they're underwater.)

'Sing loud,' says Mum, 'because the baby will hear you, and maybe it will grow faster so it can meet you.'

I've never thought about the baby meeting me. Will my baby sister like me? Will she be pleased that I, Henrietta the Great Go-Getter, am her big sister? Sometimes I can be bossy. And I've never been a big sister. I need to practise. One thing about me is I have great-go-get-it determination.

'Enough singing now,' I say. I don't want to hurry my baby sister, after all. First I need to practice being a big sister.

I squeeze through the hole in my fence and skip down the street to Eloise's house. Eloise is only two years old. I can practice being a big sister with Eloise.

Eloise is in her garden, in the sand pit.
She's filling cups with sand and pouring the
sand out again. I sit in the sand with Eloise.
She's happy to see me. Little girls always
like big girls.

I say, 'How about we build a sandcastle
together?'

Eloise is excited about my idea. Already
I'm being a good pretend big sister. But
Eloise stomps on my sandcastle. She thinks
this is very funny. Obviously, you can't
expect little sisters to respect sandcastles.
I've already learned something.

After that, Eloise wants to play Ring a Ring a Rosie. She especially likes the bit when we both fall down. She says, 'Again?' So we do it again.

And again. And again. Until finally I say, 'No more.' Enough is enough. There are only so many times you can play.

But then Eloise starts to cry. In fact she begins to wail and stomp, and soon she's screaming and getting red in the face. She turns into a terrible monster, right before my eyes. It's like magic. *Sheeza mageeza!* Am I in big trouble?

Her mum comes and picks her up, but she isn't cross. She says, 'Eloise is very tired, that's all.'

Well, as a matter of fact, I'm very extremely tired, too, but it doesn't turn me into a monster. I am still me. It's hard work practicing to be a big sister. I trudge home. It looks like I'm not quite ready for a baby sister.

But at least I've learned some patience. Now I know I can wait half way to Christmas. The apples can grow as slowly as they like. I can wait for the buds in spring. Patience isn't as hard as I thought.

When I walk in our door, I smell chocolate ripple cake. And it's ready right now! No waiting necessary.

The First Day

If you're wondering why I'm known as
Henrietta the Great Go-Getter,
it's because of my adventurous spirit and
my **great** determination. I'm an explorer
of life, and that includes trees, bugs,
animals and all mysteries.

But, I should warn you, the truth is I'm really very shy. If you met me you would see. Here's a secret. Shy people pretend they're great adventurers so that no one knows how shy they really are.

I'm going to school. For the very first time. **My first day.**

I have a new lunch box with a cheese sandwich in it. I wanted peanut butter, but peanut butter is dangerous for allergic kids so you can't have it at school.

Imagine being slayed by a peanut!
Better to **fight** a dragon or get captured
by a flying saucer.

Last night I shined my shoes with Mum's hairspray. Mum said hairspray is for making shiny hair, not shiny shoes. Oh well. Now I know. Mum showed me the shoe polish in a round tin.

It smelled worse than hairspray but it worked better. I like the way my shoes look ready for school. And I like the way I have a new pack with my lunch box ready inside. I am ready all over.

Or am I?

Now that all the preparing is done, I'm suddenly not so sure. After all, I have a nice house here with doors to slam, and a biscuit tin on the top shelf, and a hole in the fence for sneaking through, and a garden with an apple tree.

What more does a kid need?

'Mum, I don't want to go to school today. I'd rather stay home and play games with you.'

Mum says, 'But Henrietta, I know you'll really like school once you're used to it.'

And I say, 'No, actually, I think I already like the way things are here. So I might just go and hide in the cupboard now.'

While I'm hiding in the cupboard, waiting for Mum to find me, I try to imagine what school will be like. Will I have to sit still all day long? Will I get into trouble if I wriggle even a little bit? Will there be bullies and mean kids?

I hear a knock on the cupboard door. Mum has found me.

'Are you in there?'

'No.'

Mum says, 'Well that's a shame because I've thought up a game that Henrietta would love to play, if only I could find her.'

I pop my head out. 'Look! Surprise, surprise. Here I am after all.'

Mum whispers, 'How about we play spies? We can walk to school and just have a secret peep inside.'

Mum sometimes does have excellent ideas. Spying on school. Imagine.

'But I'll be the head spy?'

'Yes,' says Mum.

'And then we come home again?'

'Yes,' says Mum. 'Then we come home.'

On the way we see a spider web with a bee
stuck in it. Since I'm the head spy, I hatch a
plan free the bee at once. Spies are obliged
to perform rescues whenever they can.
Especially if it's to rescue a honey-making
creature.

So we unstick the bee and watch
it fly away. It forgets to say thank you.
That's how it is in nature.

Then we meet the lollipop lady.
She wears a yellow coat and holds a sign
like this:

Her name is Beverly. She makes us stand
behind the line until she blows her whistle.
She's like a sergeant major.

Mum whispers to me, 'At school there
are rules.'

Obviously, we need to practise standing behind the line like real school children. We pretend to be obedient, but really we're secret spies trying to uncover secrets.

So I have to poke my shiny shoe a tiny bit over the line, just to see what Beverly will do. Will she explode?

But she's too busy telling other kids to stand behind the line. You can see she likes the sergeant major job.

When we get to school there's a hook with my name on it, outside the classroom.

I do like a hook that's ready and waiting just for me. But it doesn't say 'Henrietta the Great Go-Getter', it only says 'Henrietta Hopkins'. Since we're just spying, I won't correct the hook. Not yet.

We peek around the door. There is not one single kid I know.

How can I play with kids I don't know? Even spies feel shy. What a conundrum, which, if you don't know, is a tangled-up situation that can't quite be untangled. My mum sneaks us inside the classroom.

We're undercover. I stand next to Mum and pretend I'm busy. I count the crayons in a box. Spies always count things. I think of my apple tree at home. I think about the teacher with her black curly hair and round glasses. Will she make me eat zucchini, or check I brushed my teeth, or tell me my hair is in knots?

She says, 'Hello. Who have we got here?'

I say, 'I'm not staying at school. We're just looking, thank you.'

My mum says, 'This is Henrietta.'

The teacher says, 'Henrietta, maybe you'd like to stay for a little while?'

'No thank you. I'm going home very soon. We have some rescues to do,' says I.

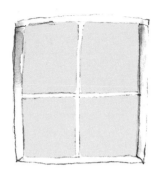

Just then someone starts to cry. It's a girl
with plaits. She's wearing denim shorts and
carrying a wombat. She doesn't want to stay
at school, either, but her mum has left her
here. I wouldn't like that. I hold my mum's
hand, just to make sure.

The teacher tries to comfort the girl. If I was that girl I wouldn't feel comforted by a grown-up I'd never ever met before, even if she was the kindest person in the world.

I have a good idea.

I will comfort the crying girl because I'm new, just like her, and I know exactly how she feels. And I know how to perform rescues because I'm a secret spy who has already rescued a bee.

I let go of Mum's hand, walk up close and say, 'Hello.'

The girl looks at me. She's still crying, so she can't say hello back, but I understand. So I say, 'Would you like to come and see the crayons with me?'

She nods.

I hold her hand and take her over to the crayon box. 'Let's write our names on pieces of paper,' I say.

She stops crying now. She looks astonished.

She says, 'But I can't write yet.'

And I say, 'That's not one bit of a problem because I can't either, so let's draw our houses instead.'

We start drawing our houses.

Soon the crying girl is having a nice time. She even asks me a question.

'What's your name?'

'Henrietta Hopkins,' I say, so as not to frighten her with my title. 'What's yours?'

'Olive Higgie.'

'That rhymes with piggy,' I say. And then I chuckle. And luckily Olive Higgie chuckles too. It's important to have a sense of humour when you're at school for the first time.

My mum says, 'Do you want to come home now, Henrietta?' And I whisper to her that I'm afraid I'll have to stay at school and look after Olive Higgie, as it's her first day and she's very shy and doesn't know anyone else except ME. Spies have to look after frightened people. It's a rescue mission.

Mum agrees that this is an important job. And after she leaves, Olive Higgie and I start to draw pigs on the piece of paper. Like this:

We draw all kinds of animals, even made-up ones. **Like this:**

We're having such a good time we almost forget it's our first day of school and we're very shy and there are rules.

The teacher says, 'It's time to begin. Come and sit in a circle.' Our first rule.

Olive Higgie and I sit next to each other. Let me share another secret.

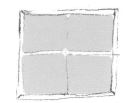

You only need one friend in a
room full of strangers to feel perfectly
happy. To tell the truth, since truth is
something I like to tell, I don't know
if I rescued Olive Higgie, or if she
rescued me, or if we rescued each
other, but now perhaps I will like
school after all.

The Sleepover

Sheeza mageeza. You'll never guess.

I'm invited to my friend Olive Higgie's house for a sleepover. Me, Henrietta the Great Go-Getter. I have never ever in my life been for a sleepover.

But don't worry, I'm not one bit nervous. I'm extremely excited. And I have a sleeping bag with leopard skin on the inside. Just hear me roar.

I pack all the things I'll need. My spotty pyjamas, of course. Mr Nelson, who is my knitted monkey, only for in bed at night. My toothbrush for keeping the dentist away, and my hairbrush because Olive Higgie does like to play hairdressers.

My secret diary because I may want to write something secret at any moment. My gumboots in case we go out stomping in the rain. And my sleeping bag, of course. My hula hoop in case I want to put on a circus. But the hula hoop won't actually fit in the bag.

Never mind, I'll just carry it along anyway.

Mum says, 'What about clean clothes for tomorrow?'

Tomorrow? I always forget to think about tomorrow. Hula hoops are more important than tomorrow.

Olive Higgie's house is green. There's
a ginger cat in the front garden. Olive Higgie
comes to the door. She's just as excited as I
am. She has made apricot slice for afternoon
tea, and even set the table with lavender
in the middle. We sit at the table, eating
apricot slice for afternoon tea, like two ladies.

I wave goodbye to Mum. I'm not one bit
sad to see her leave. I feel quite grown-up
now that I'm having my first sleepover.

Olive Higgie has an older brother called
Max. He does disgusting things like pulling
apart dead cockroaches in front of us when
we're trying to eat apricot slice. He also
likes to throw things (cockroaches, rotten
plums, water bombs) at us. Or wrestle.
Or spy on us. But we always catch him.

'Max. We can see you're spying on us,'
calls Olive Higgie.

Then she whispers to me,
'Let's do something
very, very secret,
and we won't
let Max see.'

This is a fine plan. But what?

It will soon be bedtime, so we decide to hide Max's pyjamas. But where?

'Let's hang them in a tree, like a scarecrow,' I say.

Olive Higgie giggles into her hand.

This is an equally fine idea. We sneak into Max's bedroom on tip toes.

Olive Higgie slips her hand under his pillow and pulls out his pyjamas. They're blue and stripy and all crinkled up like a piece of paper. She passes me the legs half, and we stick them under our tops and sneak out like fat secret agents.

But how to hang them in the tree?

Olive Higgie says, 'Pegs will do it.'

So we peg Max's pyjamas in the tree, just like a scarecrow. The birds all fly away fast. They must think there's a pyjama monster in their tree. Poor birds.

'What if the birds want to come home to

their nests at bedtime, but they're frightened
of the pyjama monster?' I ask.

Olive Higgie considers this. I do like to
think of a problem and then see if Olive
Higgie can figure it out. She's pretty good
at figuring.

'Well,' she says, 'we'll take down the pyjama monster before it gets dark, but leave it there until Max thinks his pyjamas have run away.'

'Ha, ha, runaway pyjamas,' says I.

'He, he, stinky pyjama monster,' Olive says.

We have a good laugh and then we make up a silly hula hoop dance, which we perform for all the birds who have flown off to trees without pyjama monsters in them.

'They don't say thank you, but that's how it is in nature.

All that hula hooping makes us hot and tired. We change into our bathers and pretend the bathtub is a cool swimming pool. We lie on our backs and let our hair spread out under the water like mermaids.

Olive Higgie says, 'I wouldn't really like to be a mermaid, because I wouldn't want a fish's tail. I do like running around and jumping on the trampoline.'

'Yes,' I agree. 'And breathing air and sleeping in beds and stomping, skipping, skylarking...'

I'm rudely interrupted by Max, who pokes his head around the door. Then he runs out, shouting through the house, 'Ha, ha, the girls think they're mermaids,' as if it's silly to pretend to be mermaids. But we have our own opinions about that, and we don't care one bit what boys think. We only act like we do, just for fun.

'Hmmmph,' I say, haughty as possible, 'There is such a thing as privacy.'

'Big brothers are so annoying,' agrees Olive Higgie. 'But just wait till he can't find his pyjamas. Then he'll be sorry.'

And we start to laugh again. Laughing mermaids are the very best sort. Much better than weeping ones who sit on rocks and wish they could walk.

After that it's dinnertime. We're wearing our pyjamas already. We've combed our hair one hundred times. We smell like roses because we put cream all over us after the bath, like ladies. But I can also smell dinner.

What if it's brussels sprouts, or pink fish with bones, or green salad? Things I don't like. I'm a little nervous all of a sudden, because at other people's houses you're not allowed to complain. What if it's brussels sprout salad? I'll come out in spots if I have to eat that.

'Olive,' I whisper, 'what are we having for dinner?'

Olive goes on a mission of discovery. 'Lentil soup? Do you like it?'

'Well, it's much better than brussels sprouts.' I don't say I would have preferred peanut butter sandwich, because that would be rude.

At dinner, I watch Max to see if he suspects his pyjamas have been stolen. But Max is busy boasting about the Magpies, which is his football team. My dad barracks for the Tigers. I just barrack for me and the small creatures, which I do like to rescue whenever I can. It's important to stand up for small things. My mum says it's also important to eat vegetables, and to be kind. I eat nearly all my lentil soup, and I don't tell Max that his football team is a dud, because I'm trying to be kind.

And guess what we have for dessert?

Apple crumble! I'm particularly fond of apple crumble.

Finally it's bedtime. Finally Max is told
to put his pyjamas on. Olive Higgie and
I keep the straightest of faces. We wait. We
keep waiting. Max comes out. He's wearing
different pyjamas. Red ones with racing cars.
I look at Olive Higgie and Olive Higgie looks
at me. We're very disappointed. Max doesn't
even realise his other pyjamas have run away.

'What are you staring at?' he says to Olive.

'Nothing,' she says.

'Yes, nothing,' I add.

Max puts Olive in a headlock and I try
to pull him off and we end up in a big fight
on the carpet, which is quite good fun.

But once we're in bed, we debrief.

'The problem is boys don't notice
pyjamas. Next time, we'll have to put some
worms in his bed. Boys notice worms.'

Olive Higgie knows more about boys
than I do.

'Would he notice if we put slime in his
bed?' I ask.

'Yes,' she yawns. 'Slime and worms...'

Olive Higgie falls asleep very quick sticks.
But I'm still awake. Olive Higgie's bedroom
is not my bedroom, and I'm not in my bed,
and usually my mum plays a song on her
ukelele to help me go to sleep. I wish my
mum was here, playing me a song. Maybe
'Summertime'. That's her favourite.

I look out the window. It's dark outside. I feel all alone. Now I'm not so sure sleepovers are a good idea. There's a whispery, black tree right near the window, full of shadowy things and – Sheeza Mageeza!

I jump onto Olive Higgie's bed and wake her up.

'There's someone in the tree! I'm scared.'

Olive Higgie sits straight up in her bed and looks out the window. Then she giggles.

'Henrietta, it's only our pyjama monster. We forgot to get it down.'

I giggle, too. Then we're both giggling so much that Max comes running in and says, 'What's going on?'

Olive Higgie points out the window. 'Your pyjamas, they're standing in the tree. Look!'

And I say, 'You better get them because otherwise the birds won't fly home to their nests!'

Max looks. We can tell he isn't keen on fetching his pyjamas, but he doesn't want us to see he's scared of the dark. So he runs out there as fast as he can, pulls his pyjamas down and comes back in, white as a ghost. Then he headlocks me and Olive Higgie tries to pull me out and we all end up fighting on the carpet.

I'm tired after all that fighting, but we're very pleased we did get even with Max, after all.

Olive Higgie sings me 'Old MacDonald had a Farm', instead of 'Summertime', even though it's the world's most boring song. I only hear the first verse because it sends me to sleep. Instantly.

The School Play

We're doing a school play. All our parents are invited. We'll dress up in costumes and be proper actors and actresses. It's hard to stop thinking about it. I'm enormously excited, to tell the truth.

I've had a lot of practice at pretending to be someone else. That's what acting is. Sometimes I'm a dragon, breathing fire and waving my thorny tail, scaring the butterflies, and sometimes I'm singing lullabies to the apples in the apple tree. So I'll definitely be a good actress, but the problem is that Olive Higgie is even more excited than me, because when Olive Higgie grows up she's going to be a famous actress and I'm going to be an explorer.

Explorers can't be actresses as well, so I have to let Olive Higgie be more excited than me, which is hard because I'd like to be the most excited of anyone.

Our school play will be an adventure story about a man called Noah who gets all the animals on his boat before a flood comes. I would very much like to be Noah in the play, as he's the most important person in the story. He's the hero. And I also have heroic qualities, because I'm fond of a rescue.

We're sitting in a circle. The teacher has a list of who will be who in the play. I'm crossing my fingers. I don't want to be a camel, that's for sure. Camels don't make any noise. The teacher says, 'Henrietta, you will be a bat.' Then she says, 'Olive Higgie, you will be Noah.' And then she says, 'Harry Binch, you will be a camel.'

Harry Binch is very quiet, so he won't mind being a camel.

Olive Higgie is very proud and pleased

to be Noah. She claps her hands loudly. I'm a bit quiet about being the bat. I can't speak to Olive Higgie straight away, because I'm full of jealousy. It's much more special to be Noah than to be a bat. Everyone will be watching Noah. Not the bat. But at least I'm not the camel, and bats can hang upside down. Also, since Olive Higgie is my best friend, I must try to be happy for her and not sad for me. It's always much nicer to happy with someone than it is to be full of bad feelings.

So I turn to Olive Higgie and I say, 'Congratulations, Olive. You'll be the best Noah.'

And she says, 'Thank you, Henrietta.
You are the only person in the class who is
good at hanging upside down.'

This is true. I am a **very good upside-
down-hanger**. I hang on the monkey bars.
So I can feel a bit proud of being a bat,
after all. And Olive and I can be pleased
together, which is important when you're
best friends.

The next day we start rehearsing. Olive
Higgie has a lot of lines to say because
Noah tells all the animals to come two by

two into the boat. But I get to say my lines while hanging upside down. Also, it doesn't take long before I add some **flying** and **swooping moves**, so the audience will be sure to see that I'm a bat. I can tell our teacher is impressed with my enthusiasm for the role, though she does keep telling me not to block off the other animals while I'm swooping.

After a while of rehearsing I realise I'm very good at being a bat, and I'm really glad I'm not Noah. I can have fun swooping and flying and hanging and beating my wings. Poor Olive Higgie must stand up straight and always be saying things.

After school Olive Higgie is quiet. Probably she's tired after all that talking. I try to cheer her up by performing some very swirly bat swoops, but this makes her even more uncheerful. Then she begins to cry, so I stop swooping. My advice is, never clown around when your friend is upset. I sit next to her and I say, 'What's wrong?'

She says, 'Well, actually, it's hard to be Noah because I'm afraid I'll never remember all the lines. And I really want to do a good job or I'll never be a famous actress.'

What a conundrum. I have a think about it.

'Olive, how about I help you learn your lines? I can pretend to be all the animals, even the camel, and you can practice saying things to me. We can do it after school or at lunch time.'

Olive Higgie opens her sad eyes wide.
She smiles.

'That would be very helpful,' she says,
and I can tell she feels better already.

The next day we begin our hard work,
though it's much harder for Olive than for
me. I enjoy pretending to be all the animals,
even the camel. Some more advice I have is,
if you ever have to be a camel, just chew a
lot and stretch your neck long. After a while
I know Olive's lines as well as Olive does,

because I happen to have an excellent memory, which makes me the perfect friend to learn with. And I'm not just making that up, because Olive Higgie says to me, 'Henrietta, you are the best best friend.'

I feel much better about being a best best friend than I would have felt being Noah. What's more, my mum helps me make a really swishy bat suit. This is how I look. Very battish indeed. I do like a black cloak. Bats are really very special and mysterious and different from regular animals. Which is a bit like me.

Today's the day of the play. Our costumes are all hanging on our school hooks. I'm swooping around the classroom in anticipation. Our teacher tells me to settle down, but bats prefer to settle up. We practise the song we're going to play on our recorders.

Finally it's time to put on our costumes. Harry Binch looks perfect as a camel. He has a nice hump made of cushions. And everyone likes my bat costume. Poor Olive Higgie only gets to dress like a man, which is not so exciting, but never mind.

Then all our parents begin to arrive. We wait backstage, which is outside. Just then something terrible happens. Olive Higgie has to sit down. She's pale with fright. Stage fright. She can't even move. Our teacher looks most concerned. She says, 'Class, it looks like Olive Higgie won't be able to perform today, which means we may have to cancel our play.'

Imagine the groaning and moaning when we hear that!

Our teacher says, 'I'm sorry. This is disappointing for you, after your hard work...'

Then Olive Higgie calls out in a wobbly voice, 'Henrietta knows my lines. She could be Noah.'

Everyone looks at me. I look at everyone. For a moment my head spins. Suddenly everyone is depending on me. It will be terrible to let them down. And I do have heroic qualities, after all. Besides, I want the play to go on.

'Okay, I will be Noah,' I say.

Then there's cheering and hooting and
I have to change quickly out of my swishy
bat costume and into Olive's boring Noah
costume. And before I even have a chance to
feel shy I'm walking onto the stage and I'm
saying the first words of the play: 'Welcome
to the story of Noah's Ark. I am Noah...'

So the play goes on. And when it's time
for the bat to appear, who should swoop in
but Olive Higgie, who has recovered from
her stage fright. Lucky I have an excellent
memory so I don't forget any words, and
lucky I've had a lot of practice being dragons

so I'm quite a natural at being Noah. And
at the end of the play all the parents are
clapping and clapping and I'm taking a nice
big bow.

Afterwards, everyone tells me I did a very
good job. My dad says he's proud of me,
and my mum says it's no wonder I'm such a
good Noah, because I've had a lot of practice
rescuing animals from natural disasters.

And then Olive Higgie says quietly,
'You'll be a better actress than me because I
get stage fright and you don't.'

But I say, 'I'd still rather be an explorer, and discover undiscovered things.'

And she says, 'Maybe I'll explore with you.'

And I say, 'Most certainly you can.'

And after that we both do some excellent bat swooping around the bare winter trees, until it's time to go home.

The Arrival

We're going on a special weekend away,
to our cousin's farm, to see the baby lambs.
It will be a long drive but I won't complain
because I'm enormously happy about going
there. Dad has cooked popcorn for the trip.
We'll play all my favourite songs in the car,
and watch the scenery, and look out for
horses in fields. And windmills.

We'll stay the night, so I'll pack my purple backpack and take my leopard skin sleeping bag. I'd like to take my hula hoop to show my cousins how well I can hula around, but Mum says it will take up too much room in the car. Actually, it's Mum who will take up too much room, as she has a **very large stomach** with my baby sister growing inside, but I don't tell her that as you shouldn't talk about the size of anyone's stomach, especially if they're a grown-up.

Dad packs a lot of food. He has made lasagne for dinner. I LOVE lasagne and lasagne loves me. My cousins will be very happy to see me and the lasagne. The cousins are called Verity and Tom. Verity is bigger than me and Tom is littler, so that makes it fair. Verity can already ride a horse, though, and I'd really like to ride a horse too. Mum says Verity might teach me this time. Olive Higgie will be jealous of me if I ride a horse. I can't wait to tell her. I'll ask Mum to take a photo of me in action on the horse, when it's galloping over a fallen tree.

We squeeze everything into our little red car, and Mum says she hopes it won't break down as it's a very old car that does sometimes like to break down. Dad says cars only do that when you don't expect them to, so as long as we all expect our car to break down it certainly won't.

'How long do we have to keep expecting it to break down for?' I ask. I would rather think about other things, like galloping off on a horse. Dad says he thinks we've all expected it enough now. So instead we decide to sing 'Row Row Row Your Boat', in rounds.

Outside the window the world passes by. It's a nice feeling to be going somewhere. It's what I call an adventure. You can't be sure what will happen, the spirit of adventure wiggles around inside you and it begins to sing. It sings of horses and lambs and fields of flowers, as it's springtime now and flowers are peeking out everywhere.

'Who wants popcorn?' shouts Dad. He
has the spirit of adventure in him too.

'Me!' says I. I throw some pieces out the
window when no one is looking, just like
Hansel and Gretel.

Soon we're in the countryside. There are
cows in the fields. There's a rabbit
scampering into the bushes. There are farms,
which sell things on the roadside. We read

the signs. One says Potatoes for Sale, another says Daffodils, Two Dollars a Bunch, and the next one just says Puppies.

Puppies! Hey, wait a minute. Stop the car. Puppies! I want to see them. Dad stops the car. He looks at Mum.

Mum says, 'As long as you're happy just to look. We can't get a puppy now.'

I've already jumped out of the car. 'Come on,' I say.

An adventure wouldn't be an adventure if
you didn't stop along the way to look at
puppies. Mum takes a long time to get out
of the car because of her roly poly belly.

We knock on the door and a woman
opens it. She's a bit roly poly herself. She
takes us to her laundry and opens the door.
There's a whole basket full of puppies,
black and brown, and I want to cuddle them
immediately.

When I kneel down, the puppies climb all over me. I'm like a waterfall of puppies. I'm covered with wet noses and soft ears and sharp little teeth. But there's a brown one in the corner that doesn't come close. It just looks at me.

'Come here...' I whisper, and I pat my knee very charmingly. It comes closer. I pat my knee again. Suddenly it bounds forward. I pick it up and give it a big snuggle. It nibbles my ear.

'Oh, if only I could take one home, this is the one I'd take.' I say this with a long, sad sigh. A sigh full of drama.

But Mum has had to sit down. And she's talking to Dad. And no one is paying me any attention at all. No one has even heard my long, sad sigh. The roly poly woman says, 'I reckon you're going to have a baby to take home, very soon.'

Then Dad says, 'Henrietta, I'm afraid we won't make it to the cousins. We have to take Mum home to have our baby. The baby is ready to come.'

'Now?'

Can it be true? Right in the middle of my adventure. This baby sister is very annoying. She's going to ruin my whole weekend. Now I'll never learn to ride a horse. Dad can see I'm disappointed.

'It will be exciting. You'll see. And we can go to the cousins another time soon, with our new baby.'

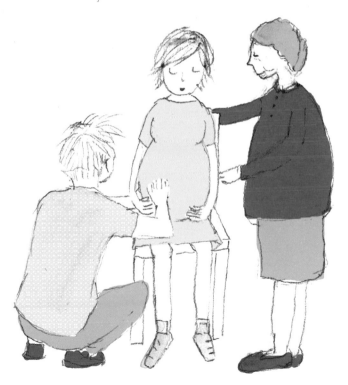

Somehow, I get the feeling this new baby is going to take up everyone's attention. Somehow, I'm not sure I want a baby sister after all. Even worse, now I have to say goodbye to my favourite brown puppy.

We get back in the car. Mum is having pains. Dad is driving fast. I'm eating popcorn and feeling miserable.

When we get home, Dad runs the bath
and calls the midwife. At least I'm allowed
to watch a movie for once, because everyone
else is preparing for the baby to come. But
the baby takes all day, and Dad and I eat
the lasagne all by ourselves. Mum is too
busy having a baby, so she can't eat. Dad
is also pretty busy helping her have a baby.
And even I start to feel a little bit excited at
the thought of meeting my new baby sister.

Finally the baby arrives. Dad calls me in and
tells me to come close. Mum is holding the
baby. It looks all red and squished-up.

'Is that my baby sister?' I say.

'No, sweetheart, this is your baby brother,'
says Mum. 'This is Albert.'

Oh boy! A baby brother. No wonder
he's all red and squishy. I didn't want a baby
brother. And already he has ruined my
weekend. I sure hope he won't make a habit
of it. I'm about to complain. I open my
mouth, but then I see how happy my mum
is, and how happy my dad is.

All their happiness comes straight at me,
so I close my mouth and smile.

You just can't be sad when everyone else
is happy, even if you didn't get to ride a
horse or keep a puppy. Even though it's
Albert who has arrived and not Alberta.

Mum tells me to sit down and she puts
Albert in my arms.

'Hello, Albert,' I say and I give him a
kiss. 'Welcome to the whirly old world.'

Albert doesn't even blink. He just says,
'Waaaaaaaaaa.'

Dad and I leave Mum and Albert to have
a big sleep together, and we go outside just
before dark. The apple tree has its new buds.
Dad was right when he said the baby would
come when the tree got its buds. It's a nice
warm night for a baby to come. Dad asks

me if I'm pleased to have a baby brother.
I have a think about this.

'It's strange that there's someone else to
think about now in our family,' I say.

'Soon you'll have someone else to play
with, too,' says Dad.

'When will he be old enough to play with?'

'After two Christmases.'

'That's even longer than waiting for him to be born!'

'True,' says Dad. 'But it went quickly, didn't it?'

I don't answer him. I can't even remember if it went quickly. The stars are beginning to shine in the sky. I feel as if life has just changed, as if one moment ago it was like I always was and now it's forever-after different. Now there's an Albert in our house. It's a funny feeling. A feeling as special and mysterious as stars.

Dad says, 'But because two years is a long time to wait, I thought maybe you and I should take a drive next weekend...'

'Where will we go?'

'We'll go get that brown puppy. Make sure you've got someone to play with till Albert is old enough.'

I jump up and down. I'm over the moon.
What a night. What a perfect night.
Now I'll have someone to look after, just
like Mum and Dad. They can look after
Albert, and I'll look after my brown puppy.

About the Author

Martine Murray was born in Melbourne. She has studied acrobatics, dance, yoga and writing. In addition to her Henrietta books, she has written two picture books, illustrated one, and written four novels that have sold extensively overseas. *Molly and Pim and the Millions of Stars* was shortlisted in the Children's Book Council of Australia's Book of the Year Award: Younger Readers.